For Jennifer, Adam and Amy
C.H.
For Rachel and Carolyn
F.K.

Text copyright © 1992 by J. M. Dent & Sons, Ltd.
Illustrations copyright © 1992 by Claire Henley.
The right of Claire Henley to be identified as the illustrator of this
work has been asserted by her in accordance with the Copyright,
Designs and Patents Act 1988.
All rights reserved. Printed in Italy.

First published 1992 by J. M. Dent & Sons, Ltd, 91 Clapham High
Street, London SW4 7TA.

The illustrations for this book were prepared using gouache paints.

FIRST U.S. EDITION
1 3 5 7 9 10 8 6 4 2

Library of Congress Cataloging-in-Publication Data

Henley, Claire.
In the ocean/by Claire Henley—1st ed.
p.   cm.
Summary: Introduces animals found in or around the sea,
including the dolphin, octopus, and penguin.
ISBN 1–56282–153–9. trade—ISBN 1–56282–154–7 (lib. bdg.)
1. Marine fauna—Juvenile literature. [1. Marine animals.]
I. Title.
QL 122.2.H47 1992
591.92—dc20

91–25905
CIP
AC

In the Ocean

Claire Henley

Hyperion Books for Children
New York

Waves lap over the yellow sand.
Seaweed and shells are stranded
on the shore.

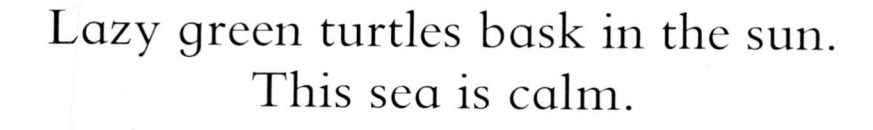

Lazy green turtles bask in the sun.
This sea is calm.

Dolphins leap and twist in
the deep blue waves.

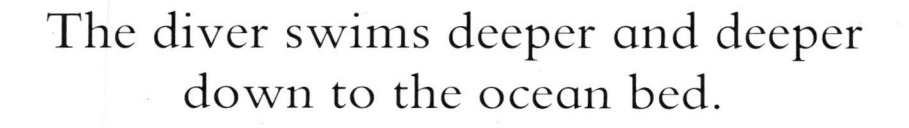

The diver swims deeper and deeper
down to the ocean bed.

Tiny rainbow-colored fish dart
through the coral reef.

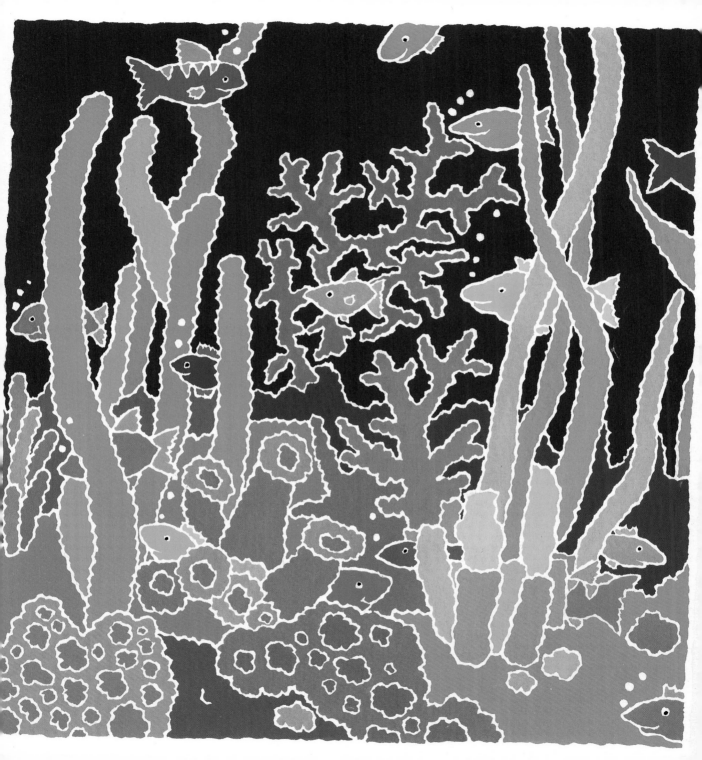

Jellyfish glide.
Nearby, a long-legged octopus
twists and twirls.

Seahorses and starfish float past.
Sea anemones sway in the warm water.

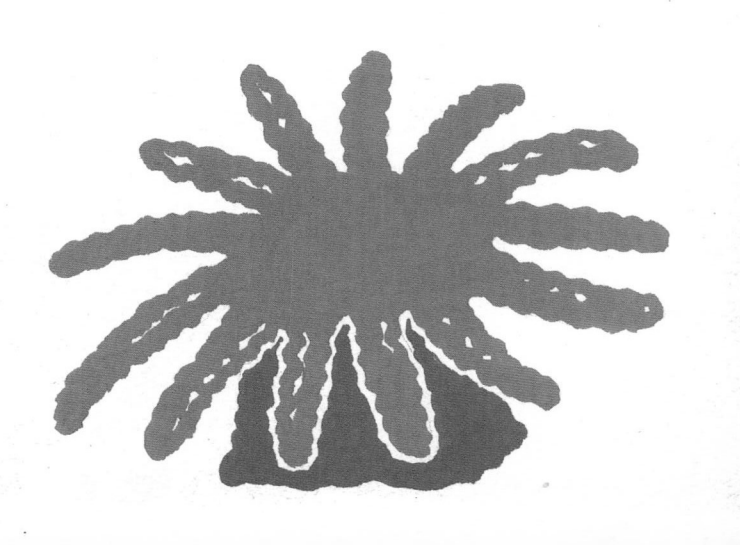

In a different, faraway harbor
a ship is ready to sail to distant stormy
seas.

Seagulls swoop and screech over
the foaming water, looking for food.

Huge whales spout
fountains of water high
into the sky.

Bright orange-beaked penguins dive
off the jagged icebergs.

The suns sets on the watery horizon.
The captain and his crew set a course for
home.